Billy's Book

Terry Bisson

Transreal Books
2020

Billy's Book
Text-only Paperback, © Terry Bisson 2020
Print ISBN: 978-1-940948-49-2
Cover by Lisa Roth

Billy's Book
Illustrated Ebook, © Terry Bisson 2020
ISBN: 978-1-940948-47-8

Billy's Picture Book
Illustrated Paperback, © Terry Bisson 2020
Print ISBN: 978-1-940948-46-1

Transreal Books
2020

Special thanks to
Rudy Rucker
my Partner in Crime

Contents

Billy and the Ants

It was a beautiful morning.
"Die!" said Billy.
The ants were marching in a long row, up the driveway toward the garage.
"Rat-a-tat-tat!" said Billy, making a machine-gun noise as he slid his shoe along the concrete.
The ants died, ten at a time.
"What are you doing?" Billy's mother asked.
"Playing," said Billy.

There was a drain at the bottom of the driveway.
Billy got his water gun.
"Flash flood!" he said, washing the ants down the drain. They tried to swim but it did them no good.
"Stay out of the street," said Billy's mother.
"Yes, ma'am," said Billy. He knew better than to go into the street.

"Oh boy," said Billy. These ants were bigger.
"Boom boom boom," he said, making an artillery-noise as he hit them with the hammer.
Each ant left a little spot on the concrete.
"Is that your father's good hammer?" asked Billy's mother. "Put it back."

"Where are you going with that steak knife?" asked Billy's mother.

"Playing soldier."

"Well, don't go out of the yard."

"Yes, ma'am." There were lots of ants in the yard, by the garbage can. They were bigger than the ones in the driveway.

"Fix bayonets!" said Billy.

The ants tried to run.

"Die!" said Billy, as he stabbed them with the steak knife, one by one.

There were even more ants by the garden shed.

"Enemy sighted!" said Billy.

The ants were hiding under the grass, but it did them no good. They were almost an inch long, and easy to find.

"Bombs away!" said Billy, making an airplane noise as he dropped the bricks on them.

"Lunch!" said Billy's mother, from the house.

"In a minute," said Billy. He was looking around for more ants to kill.

"Peanut butter and jelly!" said Billy's mother.

Peanut butter and jelly was Billy's favorite.

"Coming!" he said.

"Your father called," said Billy's mother. "He's coming home tomorrow. He's bringing you a present."

"Can I have another sandwich?" asked Billy. He had a lot of ants to kill.

"May you have another sandwich," said Billy's mother. "And then it's nap time."

Billy hated naps. He lay on his bed, on top of the covers.

He heard a scratching noise outside.

He got up and looked out the window.

There was a big ant, as big as a rat. It was trying to climb up the side of the house to the window. Its feelers were waving around.

Billy got his bow and arrows out of his toy chest. The arrows had rubber tips. He pulled them off and sharpened the arrows in his pencil sharpener. It was electric.

Then Billy leaned out the window with his bow. The first arrow bounced off the ant, but the next two went all the way through and stuck out the other side.

The ant fell on its back, waving its legs in the air. The arrows looked like extra legs.

Then Billy heard his mother's footsteps. He jumped back into bed and closed his eyes.

His mother opened the door. "Are you asleep?" she whispered.

Billy knew better than to answer.

"Go play in the back yard," said Billy's mother, when his nap time was over. "I'm cleaning the house."

"Yes ma'am," said Billy. He took his bow with him.

The ant under the window was dead. Billy buried it in the sandbox so his mother wouldn't see it. First he pulled out the arrows. They were covered with yellow ant blood.

"Cool," said Billy.

He wiped them off in the grass and looked around for more ants to kill.

He didn't have to look far.

There was an ant on the seat of Billy's swing.

It was as big as a cat. It had a sharp snout and big pincers. It was waving its legs and trying to swing.

Billy shot it three times but the arrows bounced off. Then he got the pitchfork out of the garden shed and speared the ant through the middle. He pinned it to the ground and watched it die.

Billy kicked the ant's body into the bushes and swung for a while.

Then he got tired of swinging and spun around.

"Suppertime," said Billy's mother, from the house.

"In a minute," said Billy.

There was an ant between him and the back door. It was as big as a dog. He would have to kill it, but how?

Billy got the shovel out of the garden shed and raised it over his head. It was heavy and the blade was sharp.

He hit the ant twice, breaking it into three pieces. He watched from the back steps as each piece died separately.

Then he went inside to eat.

"How big do ants get?"

"How should I know?" said Billy's mother. "Eat your brussels sprouts."

"I don't like brussels sprouts," said Billy.

"Eat them anyway," said his mother. "Then you can watch TV for one hour before bed time."

Billy was watching his favorite show when he felt the couch rock, back and forth.

Uh oh, he thought.

He waited till his mother left the room, then looked behind the couch.

There was an ant, as big as a boy. It was looking up at him. Each eye was made out of lots of little eyes.

Billy grabbed a poker from the fireplace and jammed it into the ant's eyes, first one and then the other. Yellow stuff came out. After a while, the couch stopped rocking.

"What are you doing?" asked Billy's mother.

"Nothing," said Billy.

"Bed time," said Billy's mother.

There was a little hatchet by the fireplace. Billy's father used it for splitting kindling.

Billy took it to bed with him.

"May I leave the light on?" he asked.

"You know you're too big for that," said Billy's mother.

Billy's room was dark.

The house was quiet.

Something was in the closet, thumping. It sounded big.

Billy got out of bed and pushed his dresser against the closet door. It was heavy and hard to move.

It wasn't heavy enough, though. At about midnight the dresser began to slide. The closet door creaked open.

Billy hid under the covers, but the ant knew where to find him. It was as big as a man. It had a sharp snout and huge pincers. It had long hairy legs. It climbed up onto the bed and pulled at the covers with its pincers.

It pulled them off.

Billy swung the hatchet. He chopped off two legs but the ant kept coming. Billy swung again and the ant grabbed the hatchet with its sharp snout and snapped it in half.

Then it snapped Billy in half.

"Where's Billy?" asked Billy's father, the next day, when he got home.

"The ants ate him," said Billy's mother.

"Those little devils," said Billy's father. "That Billy was a nice boy. Look. I even brought him a present."
He took it out of the bag. It was an ant farm.
Billy's mother held it up to the light.
"Billy wouldn't have liked it anyway," she said. "They're all dead."

Billy and the Fairy

"There's something in my room," said Billy. "I think it's a fairy."

"Fairies are make-believe," said Billy's mother.

"It glows in the dark," said Billy.

"Go back to bed," said Billy's father.

Billy's bed was shaped like a race car. There was a little tiny person sitting on the front of the bed, beside the steering wheel.

"Are you a fairy?" Billy asked.

"Who wants to know?"

"Me," said Billy. "It's my room."

"So what," said the fairy.

Billy thought about that. "Are you really a fairy?" he asked.

"Are you really a little boy?"

"That's a stupid question," said Billy.

"You're a stupid little boy."

"What are you doing in my room? My mother says fairies are make-believe."

"They are," said the fairy. "Real fairies are. I'm not."

"I thought you said you were a real fairy."

"I never said that," said the fairy. "I'm really a fairy, but I'm not a real fairy. Real fairies are make-believe. I'm not make-believe."

"Make-believe stuff is stupid," said Billy, getting into bed. "Why aren't you wearing any pants?"

"Fairies don't have to. Who is that on your pajamas?"

"Dale Earnhardt," said Billy. "He's a race car driver."

"He looks like your father," said the fairy. "Aren't you supposed to sleep with your head at this end?"

"I'm afraid of you," said Billy.

"Suit yourself," said the fairy.

In the morning, the fairy was gone.

"Is there such a thing," Billy asked at breakfast, "as fairies?"

"Are there such a thing," his mother said.

That didn't sound right to Billy. "There's just one," he said. "He doesn't wear any pants."

"Then watch out for him," said Billy's father.

"It's OK to believe in make-believe," said Billy's mother. "Just don't confuse it with reality."

"Huh?" said Billy.

"And don't forget those leaves," said Billy's father, getting up to go.

Billy picked up the leaves out of the driveway. It was his only chore.

When he was finished, he went to his room.

He was hoping to talk to the fairy but the fairy was gone. There was a wet spot by the steering wheel, where it had sat.

When Billy went to bed, the fairy was back. It glowed in the dark, like a lightning bug.

"Where do fairies go during the day?" Billy asked.

"Real fairies? They don't go anywhere," said the fairy. "They're only make-believe. They have no place to go. No place would have them."

"Where do you go?" asked Billy.

"Wouldn't you like to know," said the fairy.

"Why do you come here?" asked Billy.

"I like this bed. It's shaped like a race car."

"You can sit on it," Billy said. "But I wish you would wear pants."

The next morning, the fairy was gone. There was a wet spot on Billy's bed.

"What if there was just one fairy?" Billy asked at breakfast. "Would that be make-believe?"

"Of course," said Billy's mother. "Every child has a right to a little make-believe."

"There you go with those rights again," said Billy's father. He patted Billy on the head, like a dog. "I guess one fairy's OK, as long as he helps you pick up those leaves out of the driveway."

"He doesn't do things," said Billy.

First Billy picked up the leaves, then he went to his room. The fairy was sitting on his bed, next to the steering wheel.

"What do fairies do?" asked Billy.

"Nothing much," said the fairy. "Sometimes we kill people."

"Huh?"

"When God wants a new angel in Heaven, sometimes He sends a fairy down to kill him. Or her."

"Are you here to kill me?" asked Billy.

"Of course not," said the fairy.

Billy thought about that. "My Mom doesn't believe in fairies," he said.

"So what," said the fairy.

"So she says you are just make-believe. That's what."

"That's because she's stupid."

"My Mom's not stupid."

"That's what you think," said the fairy.

Billy had an idea. "Wait here," he said.

Billy went into the kitchen.

"Come quick," he said. "I want to show you something."

"Not the fairy, Billy," his mother said. She was baking a pie. "Can't you see I'm busy?"

"Please, Mom," said Billy.

Billy's mother wiped her hands and followed him into his bedroom.

The fairy was gone. But that was OK.

"Look, Mom!" said Billy. He showed her the wet spot on the bed. "That's where it was sitting."

"Billy," said Billy's mother.

"Billy's growing up," said Billy's mother at dinner.

"Good. Then maybe he can do what he's told," said Billy's father. "Like pick up the leaves out of the driveway."

"But I did," said Billy.

"Sir," said his father.

"But I did, sir."

"Then where did I find this little item?" Billy's father pulled a leaf from his shirt pocket and set it on the table.

"They fall off the trees," said Billy.

Billy put on his pajamas. The fairy was sitting on the bed.

"I saw your guy today," the fairy said. "Dale Earnhardt."

Dale Earnhardt was dead. Billy had seen the crash on TV.

"No you didn't," Billy said. "And I wish you would wear pants."

"Fairies don't have to wear pants. Dale said to tell you hello."

"No, he didn't," said Billy.

"You're right, he didn't," said the fairy. "Dead people don't say hello. I did see him, though."

"Where? In Heaven?"

The fairy laughed. It made a nasty little tinkling sound.

"I didn't know him anyway," said Billy, getting into bed. "He was just famous."

Billy woke up in the middle of the night.

The fairy was still there, glowing like a lightning bug.

"Do you really kill people?" Billy asked.

"Sometimes."

"Why doesn't God send an angel down to do it?"

"Angels are make-believe," said the fairy. "I use a long needle."

Billy thought about that. "Can I see it?"

"Go back to sleep, Billy."

Billy went back to sleep.

"How's your fairy doing?" Billy's mother asked at breakfast. "Is it still there?"

"Sometimes," Billy said.

"Maybe he can help you pick up the leaves out of the driveway before I get home," said Billy's father.

"He doesn't do things," said Billy. "I told you."

"Sir," said Billy's father.

"Sir," said Billy.

Billy picked up the leaves himself. There was nothing else to do anyway. The fairy was gone all day.

"I thought you and your fairy were going to pick up the leaves out of the driveway before I got home," said Billy's father at dinner.

"But I did," said Billy. "Sir."

"Then where did I find this little item?"

"Do you really kill people?" asked Billy. He was getting ready for bed.

"You already asked me that," said the fairy. "Who do you want me to kill?"

Billy thought about that. "My father," he said.

The next morning, Billy's father slumped over at the breakfast table.

"Oh dear," said Billy's mother.

He was dead. The ambulance came and got him.

"That was cool," said Billy that night as he was putting on his pajamas. "But I didn't see any long needle."

"Of course not," said the fairy.

The next day, the fairy killed Billy's mother.

She slumped over and her face went into the pie. This time, Billy saw the long needle.

The fairy was sitting on top of the refrigerator. Its little legs were crossed.

"That was stupid," said Billy. "Now I don't have any parents."

"So what," said the fairy.

"So the police will come and put me in the orphanage. That's what."

"Not if they don't know she's dead," said the fairy.

Billy thought about that. He dragged his mother into the closet and shut the door.

"I still don't have anybody to take care of me," he said.

"Clean up the pie," said the fairy. "I'll ask around."

That night there was no supper. Billy got a box of cereal and took it to his room.

Dale Earnhardt was sitting on the bed. "Straight out of the box," he said. "Classy."

"I thought you were dead," said Billy. "I saw the crash on TV."

"Sit down, kid," said Dale Earnhardt. He stretched out on the bed. Billy sat down beside him.

"I can deal with the stiff in the closet," Dale Earnhardt said. "But you have to do your part, kid."

"What's that?"

"What's that, sir."

"What's that, sir?"

"There's the little matter of the leaves in the driveway."

Billy thought about that. He looked around for the fairy, but the fairy was gone.

There was only a wet spot where it once had been.

Billy and the Bulldozer

Billy had a bulldozer. It was yellow.
It was big enough to sit on.
Billy made a house in the sandbox. It had windows
and a door. It even had a little chimney.
Billy bulldozed it down.
Then he built it again and bulldozed it down.

"What did you do all day?" asked Billy's father. They
were eating supper.
"Played with my bulldozer," said Billy.
"Good boy," said Billy's father.
"Billy should play with his friends," said Billy's
mother. "And eat his brussels sprouts."
"Billy doesn't have any friends," said Billy's father.
"That's why I brought him that bulldozer."
"I hate brussels sprouts," said Billy.
"What did you say?" asked Billy's mother.
"Nothing," said Billy.

Billy didn't have any friends, but he had an enemy.
His name was Vernon. He lived next door.
Billy saw him across the fence. "Want to come over
and play with my bulldozer?" Billy asked.
"No," said Vernon. "Because you are stupid."

"I'm not stupid," said Billy.

"Yes you are," said Vernon. "And your bulldozer is stupid too."

Billy was afraid of storms. He heard thunder and ran into the house.

"You left your bulldozer out in the rain," said Billy's mother. "Now it will be ruined."

"No it won't," said Billy. "It's made out of metal."

"You'll see," said Billy's mother.

Billy watched out the window. It was raining on his bulldozer.

Maybe the rain really would ruin it!

Then Billy heard thunder and he closed his eyes as tight as he could.

ZZAAAAAPP!

When he opened his eyes the bulldozer was turned over.

The lightning had struck it.

"Oh no!" said Billy.

"Serves you right," said Billy's mother.

As soon as it quit raining, Billy ran outside.

The sand was already dry. Some of it had turned to glass.

Billy's bulldozer was upside down.

He turned it over. The yellow paint was brighter, where the lightning had struck it.

It was bigger than before.

Billy got on the seat and drove the bulldozer back and forth over the sand. It crunched the glass.

The lightning had made it better!

"Come see my bulldozer now," said Billy. Vernon was in his back yard, practicing spitting.

"I can see it from here," said Vernon. "And it's still stupid."

"Billy left his bulldozer out in the rain," said Billy's mother. They were eating supper.
"It's metal," said Billy's father. "It'll rust."
"Serves him right," said Billy's mother. "Eat your brussels sprouts."
"Brussels sprouts are stupid," said Billy.
"What did you say?" asked Billy's mother.
"Nothing," said Billy. He ate his brussels sprouts. "Can I be excused?"
"May you be excused," said Billy's father.
"And now it's raining again," said Billy's mother. "And he left it out again."

Billy had left his bulldozer out on purpose.
He watched through the window from his room, with a blanket over his head, just in case.
He was waiting for the lightning to strike.
Finally, it did.

The next morning, Billy ran eagerly out to play.
His yellow bulldozer was upside down again. He turned it right side up. It was bigger and brighter than ever.
"Cool," said Billy.
He climbed up on the seat and drove it back and forth.
It crunched down the side of the sandbox and then crunched over the driveway. It made a neat grinding noise.
"Hey Vernon," said Billy. Vernon was on the other side of the fence.
Vernon acted like he didn't hear.
Billy drove the bulldozer through the fence.

Vernon tried to run away but the bulldozer ran over his feet and squashed them.

"I'm sorry!" said Vernon. He was trying to stand up, but he couldn't because he didn't have any feet any more. "I'm sorry, Billy."

Billy pretended not to hear. He drove the bulldozer harder and squashed Vernon. Then he squashed Vernon's house. Vernon's parents were inside.

His little sister, too. Her name was Grace.

"What happened next door?" asked Billy's father. They were eating supper.

"Nothing," said Billy.

"It was awful," said Billy's mother. "Something squashed them all."

"It wasn't me," said Billy.

"Even the little girl," said Billy's mother. "Her name was Grace."

"It wasn't me," said Billy.

"Nobody said it was," said Billy's father. "I brought you a present. But first you have to eat your brussels sprouts."

"Deal," said Billy. He waited till his parents weren't looking and rolled them under the table. They were like little balls.

He knew his mother wouldn't see them. She never looked under the table. "What did you bring me?"

"A tank," said Billy's father. "It's metal. You can't leave it out in the rain."

"He will, though," said Billy's mother.

Billy and the Unicorn

One day Billy saw a unicorn. He could tell what it was by the big horn growing out of its head. It was standing at the edge of the woods.

"Want a unicorn?" the unicorn asked. It was white.

Billy shook his head. "Girls like unicorns," he said. "I'm a boy."

"Boys would like unicorns too," said the unicorn, "if they knew what unicorns were really like."

Billy thought about that. "What are they really like?" he asked.

"Take me home and you'll see," said the unicorn.

"You're too big," said Billy.

"Yes, but unicorns don't eat anything," said the unicorn. "Plus, we're invisible."

Billy took the unicorn home. It was hard to get it in the door. His mother couldn't see it, though.

He put it in his room and stood it in the corner. Its horn glowed in the dark.

"Turn out that light," said Billy's mother. "Go to sleep."

Cool! thought Billy. She could see the light but not the unicorn.

Billy hung a tee shirt over the unicorn's horn. It looked like a little ghost in the dark.

"Hey," said Billy.

The unicorn was going to the bathroom.

"You can't go to the bathroom in my room," said Billy.

"Too late," said the unicorn. A big blue jewel dropped down between its legs.

It was as big as a brussels sprout. It had lots of square sides.

"Pick it up," said the unicorn.

"No way," said Billy.

After a while, the blue jewel disappeared.

"Get a load of this," said Billy's father. He was reading the paper. "'Unicorn Escapes from Zoo.'"

"I thought they were make-believe," said Billy's mother.

"It went to the bathroom in my room," said Billy.

"Shut up," said Billy's father. "Go to your room. Both of you."

When Billy got back to his room, the unicorn was going to the bathroom again.

"Hey," said Billy.

"Go ahead, pick it up," said the unicorn. "It doesn't stink."

Billy picked it up. It was warm, but it didn't stink.

"It's like money," said the unicorn. "You can buy magazines with it."

Billy liked magazines. He went to the store and picked one out.

"Dale Earnhardt," said the store owner. "That's a special memorial issue. Got any money?"

Billy shook his head.

"Then you're out of luck," said the store owner. "He was one of the Greats."

"This is like money," said Billy. He showed the store owner the blue jewel. It was still warm.

The store owner sniffed it. "You get two for that," he said. He gave Billy another magazine. It was all about girls.

"I don't like girls," said Billy.

"Give it to your unicorn," said the store owner.

"Did you really escape from the zoo?" Billy asked.

"No," said the unicorn. It was looking at the girls. Billy had to turn the pages. The unicorn had no hands.

"The paper says you did."

"I planted that story," said the unicorn. "There is no zoo."

Billy thought about that.

"Turn the page," said the unicorn.

"I thought you didn't like girls," said Billy.

"These aren't wearing any clothes," said the unicorn. "It's their clothes I don't like."

"Can I ride on your back?" Billy asked.

"After you go to bed," said the unicorn.

That night Billy rode the unicorn around the yard. Its horn was like a headlight. It left little tracks in the sandbox.

"How come my mother can't see you?" Billy asked.

"She never tried," said the unicorn. "Plus, unicorns are invisible."

"How come I can see you, then?"

"We're not that invisible," said the unicorn.

Billy thought about that. "Can I take you to school?" he asked.

"Unicorns don't like school," said the unicorn.

Billy was watching TV when the phone rang.
It was the store owner. "I want my magazines back,"
he said. "That jewel disappeared."

"It's like money," said Billy.

"Money doesn't disappear," said the store owner.
"Bring back my magazines or I will call the FBI."

"I'm not afraid of the FBI," said Billy.

But he was. His hands were trembling as he hung
up the phone.

"Who was that?" asked Billy's mother.

"Nobody," said Billy.

"Where's my Dale Earnhardt magazine?" asked
Billy. He couldn't find it anywhere.

"I found out he's dead," said the unicorn. "So I tore
it up with my horn."

"Oh no," said Billy. "He was one of the Greats."

"Dead people don't belong in magazines," said the
unicorn.

"The store owner wants his magazines back," said
Billy. He tried to get the girl magazine back but the
unicorn was standing on it. It had sharp feet like a deer.

"You're going to get us both in trouble," said Billy.
"He'll call the FBI."

"Just turn the page," said the unicorn. "Let me
worry about him."

"Get a load of this," said Billy's father. He was
reading the paper. "'Store Owner Killed by Unicorn'."

"I thought they were make-believe," said Billy's
mother.

"It's invisible," said Billy. "It has a sharp horn."

"Shut up, both of you," said Billy's father.

"That was cool," said Billy. "But I think you should hide somewhere else." He was getting tired of the unicorn.

"I like it here," said the unicorn. "But I need another magazine. I'm finished with this one."

Billy had an idea. "You would like it at school," he said. "There are lots of girls there."

"Do they wear clothes?" asked the unicorn. "It's their clothes I don't like."

"Girls like unicorns," said Billy. "They will let you look up their dresses."

The next day, Billy took the unicorn to school. The teacher couldn't see it. The boys couldn't either.

The girls could, though. "Billy has a unicorn," they said, clapping their hands together. "Can we ride on it?"

"You can have it," said Billy. He was tired of the unicorn. "Jewels come out of its butt."

"That's cool," said the girls. "It can sleep in the girls' bathroom."

"It doesn't sleep," said Billy.

"Let's go!" said the unicorn. It took all the girls for a ride. It looked up their dresses as they got on and off.

"What's going on?" asked the boys.

Billy told them about the unicorn. "It's invisible," he said. He left out the part about the store owner.

"Invisible stuff is make-believe," said the boys. "Plus, unicorns are strictly for girls."

"Boys would like unicorns too, if they knew what they were really like," said Billy.

But the boys couldn't see it. "Billy has a unicorn," they said. "Billy the girl!"

They made fun of Billy.

This was their big mistake.

"Home from school already?" asked Billy's mother.

"They let us out early," said Billy.

"Get a load of this," said Billy's father. He was reading the paper at the supper table. "'Unicorn Kills School Boys'."

"That must be why they let Billy out early," said Billy's mother. "It was a tragedy."

"It says here that it tore them up with its horn," said Billy's father. "Then it ran into the girls' bathroom."

"Girls like unicorns," said Billy's mother.

"The teacher called the FBI," said Billy's father. "They will investigate."

"It wasn't my fault," said Billy.

"Nobody said it was," said Billy's father. "Pass the brussels sprouts."

"I'm pretty sure unicorns are make-believe," said Billy's mother.

"Boys would like unicorns too if they knew what they were really like," said Billy.

"No they wouldn't," said Billy's father. "Now shut up, both of you."

Billy and the Spacemen

"Look what I found in the driveway," said Billy's father. He held up a little rocket ship. "I almost ran over it. Does it belong to anyone here?"

"No, sir," said Billy.

"We have a problem then," said Billy's father. "It must be a spaceship from another planet."

"Is there anyone inside?" asked Billy's mother. She was carving the turkey. They had turkey every night.

Billy's father held the little rocket ship up to his ear and shook it.

"No," he said. "That means they must be hiding here in the house somewhere."

"May I be excused?" asked Billy.

"Not until you eat your turkey," said Billy's mother.

Billy went to his room and opened his drawer.

It was filled with little spacemen. They had landed in the driveway the night before. They had climbed in the window and hidden in his drawer.

Billy had pretended to be asleep but he had watched the whole thing from under the covers.

"Who are you?" asked the spacemen when Billy opened the drawer.

Billy told them. "What planet are you from?" he asked.

"Wouldn't you like to know," they said. They were wearing space helmets. "Is this Earth?"

"Yes," said Billy. "You can take off your space helmets. There's plenty of air here. It's not like the Moon."

Billy had learned about the Moon at school. There is no air on the Moon.

"Your air stinks," said the spacemen.

"It does not," said Billy.

"It does so," said the spacemen. They put their helmets back on. "We are here to conquer Earth," they said. "We are going to kill everybody and then it will smell better."

"You are too little," said Billy.

"That's why we need your help," said the spacemen.

"I'm just a little boy," said Billy.

The next morning the spacemen were still in the drawer.

"Look what we found," they said.

"That's just a pencil," said Billy.

"It is not, it's a spear," said the spacemen. "Sharpen it for us."

Billy stuck the pencil in his electric pencil sharpener. A little light came on when the pencil was sharp. He gave it back to the spacemen.

"I think you should go home," he said. "You can keep the pencil."

"It's a spear," said the spacemen. "And we don't care what you think. Take us to your leader. We will kill him and take his keys."

"I have to go to school," said Billy.

"That's even better," said the spacemen. "We can hide in your lunchbox."

"What if I say no?" said Billy.

"Then we'll kill you too," said the spacemen.

Billy took the spacemen to school. They were hiding in his lunchbox. It had a rocket ship on it.

"That's a stupid lunchbox," said the teacher. "That rocket doesn't look real."

"It does so," said Billy. It was embossed. "And it's full of spacemen. They intend to conquer Earth."

"That I want to see," said the teacher.

"It's your funeral," said Billy.

He opened his lunchbox. The spacemen jumped out and killed the teacher. All the kids screamed.

Pretty soon the police came. They took Billy home.

"The teacher killed himself with a pencil," said the police. "All the kids were screaming."

"It must have been a tragedy," said Billy's mother.

"It was his own fault," said Billy.

Billy went to his room. He dumped the spacemen out of his lunchbox into his drawer.

"You almost got me in trouble," he said. "That was my teacher you killed."

"That was just for practice," said the spacemen. "Now take us to your leader so we can kill him and take his keys."

"What if I say no?"

"Then we'll kill you too," said the spacemen. "But if you help us conquer Earth, we'll make you King."

"Hmmmm," said Billy. "Let me think about it."

Billy was only pretending to think about it. He didn't want to be King. He was just a little boy. But he was afraid of the spacemen. What if they killed him?

He decided to fool them.

"Okay," he said. He took the spacemen into the bathroom and put them on the toilet seat.

"What's this?" they asked. "It's round."

"The White House," said Billy. "It's supposed to be round." He picked up a toothbrush and hid it behind his back.

"Where is your leader?" asked the spacemen.

"Down there," said Billy. "Look."

The spacemen leaned over the edge and looked down.

Billy knocked them into the water with the toothbrush. Their helmets made them float. Billy flushed the toilet and they disappeared.

Then he flushed it again just to be sure.

"Get a load of this," said Billy's father. He was reading the paper. "'Spacemen Suspected in Teacher Death'."

"What spacemen?" said Billy's mother. "I never heard anything about any spacemen."

"They were little," said Billy. "But they were mean." He told his parents how he had fooled the spacemen and flushed them down the toilet. "They intended to kill us all and conquer Earth," he said.

"That was a close call," said Billy's father. "I guess we can get rid of this little rocket now."

He took out his hammer and broke it. Then he passed the turkey.

"You could have been King," said Billy's mother. "Instead you are a hero."

"No," said Billy proudly. "I'm just a little boy."

Billy and the Wizard

Billy had a secret. He liked to play with dolls. One of Billy's dolls could talk. His name was Clyde. Clyde only talked when Billy pulled his string.

One day Billy pulled his string.

"Would you like to meet the Wizard?" Clyde asked.

Billy was surprised. Clyde had never asked a question before. Billy pulled his string again.

"How about it?" Clyde asked. "How many little boys get to meet the Wizard?"

"What's he the Wizard of?" Billy asked. He pulled Clyde's string again.

"He's the Wizard of Everything," Clyde said. "And he's hiding in the garage."

"Who's he hiding from?" asked Billy. He pulled Clyde's string again.

"He's the Wizard of Everything," said Clyde. Sometimes Clyde said the same thing over and over. "And he's hiding in the garage."

Billy looked in the garage. There was nothing there but old magazines.

"I looked in the garage," said Billy. "But I didn't see any Wizard."

He pulled Clyde's string.

"Of course not," said Clyde. "He's hiding. You have to look harder."

Billy looked harder. "I still don't see any Wizard," he said. He pulled Clyde's string.

"Of course not," said Clyde. "He's hiding. You have to look harder."

Billy looked harder. He looked through all the magazines.

Finally he found one called Today's Wizard. He opened it up and there was the Wizard. He was little and flat and he wore a pointy hat.

"I am not the Wizard," he said. "Go away."

"You are so," said Billy. "I can tell by your hat."

The Wizard didn't say anything. He was just a picture. After a while, Billy turned the page.

There was the Wizard again. "How did you find me?" he asked.

"Clyde told me you were hiding in the garage," said Billy. He turned the page again.

The Wizard was the same on every page. He had a pointy beard to go with his pointy hat. "That Clyde," said the Wizard.

"Are you really the Wizard of Everything?" Billy asked.

"Turn the page," said the Wizard. Billy did. "And who told you that, my boy?"

"Clyde," said Billy.

"That Clyde," said the Wizard. "You should know better than to pull his string. Turn the page."

Billy turned the page again.

"I'm not the Wizard of Everything," said the Wizard. "Actually, I'm the Wizard of Everything Else."

Billy thought about that. "Who are you hiding from?" he asked.

"Who do you think?" asked the Wizard.

Billy turned the page. "I give up," he said.

"The Devil," said the Wizard. "Now put me back in the pile. Here comes your mother."

"Are you playing with dolls again?" asked Billy's mother. She was standing in the door of the garage.

"No ma'am,' said Billy.

"Come to supper, then."

"Billy was playing with dolls again," said Billy's mother. She was carving the turkey.

"Of course," said Billy's father. "That's because he's a sissy."

"I am not," said Billy.

"You are so," said Billy's father. "Look, I brought you another doll."

Billy took the doll to his room after supper. It was a baby doll. Billy hated it.

It had a string. Billy pulled it.

"You're a sissy," said the doll.

"I am not," said Billy. He shook the doll and pulled the string again.

"You are so," said the doll.

Billy tied the doll to a pencil. Then he got a book of matches and burned the doll up. He pulled its string so he could hear it scream.

"What are you doing in there?" asked Billy's mother.

"Nothing," said Billy.

"Playing with dolls," said Billy's father.

"Dolls are stupid," said Billy. It was the next day. He was playing with Clyde behind the garage where no one could see. "I hate dolls," he said.

"Pull my string," said Clyde.

Billy did.

"Even dolls hate dolls," said Clyde. "I would rather be a little boy like you."

"Really?" said Billy. He hugged Clyde and pulled his string again.

"Not really," said Clyde. "You're a sissy. Would you like to meet the Wizard?"

"I already did," said Billy. "And I am not a sissy."

"How many little sissies get to meet the Wizard?" asked Clyde.

Billy threw Clyde into the garbage and went to the garage to find the Wizard.

He opened Today's Wizard, and there he was in his pointy hat.

"Where's Clyde?" asked the Wizard.

"He called me a sissy," said Billy. He turned the page.

"That Clyde," said the Wizard. "I told you not to pull his string."

"I had no one else to play with," said Billy. He looked around the garage. It was dark and scary. "Can I take you outside?" he asked.

"No way," said the Wizard. "I'm in hiding."

"Why is the Devil after you?" Billy asked.

"Why do you think?" asked the Wizard.

Billy turned the page. "I give up," he said.

"He wants to steal my hat," said the Wizard. "So he can rule the world."

Billy thought about that. "What does he look like?" he asked. He turned the page.

"He looks ugly and evil," said the Wizard. "Now put me back in the pile. Here comes your mother."

"What are you doing in there?' asked Billy's mother.

"Nothing," said Billy.

"Put your dolls away and come to supper."

"Get a load of this," said Billy's father. He was reading the paper. "'Wizard Goes Into Hiding'."

"He's hiding from the Devil," Billy said.

"He's apparently not the Wizard of Everything anyway," said Billy's father. "So what's the big deal?"

"He's the Wizard of Everything Else," said Billy.

"What do you know about it?" said Billy's mother. "Eat your turkey." They had turkey every night.

Billy woke up in the middle of the night. Clyde was standing on his chest.

Billy was afraid. "I'm sorry I threw you in the garbage," he said.

"Pull my string," said Clyde.

Billy pulled his string.

"I'm sorry I called you a sissy," said Clyde. "Now hurry. Come with me! It's an emergency."

"What's the problem?" Billy asked. He pulled Clyde's string.

"The Devil is in the garage, looking for the Wizard. It's an emergency!"

It was midnight. Billy's parents were asleep.

Billy sneaked out the side door, into the garage.

The Devil was sitting on the floor, going through the magazines. He looked ugly and evil. He had a snout like a dog. He wasn't wearing any pants.

"What are you doing here?" asked Billy. Even though he knew.

"Don't bother me, kid," said the Devil. "Go play with your dolls."

"The Wizard's not here," said Billy.

"You're a liar," said the Devil. "I like that. Now go back to bed and leave me alone. I have work to do."

He started going through the magazines again.

"This is my garage," said Billy.

"It is not," said the Devil. "It's your father's. And you're a sissy."

"I am not," said Billy. "If I had a gun I would shoot you."

"Be my guest," said the Devil. Then he said something in Latin and a magic gun appeared in Billy's hand. It was silver. Billy pointed it at the Devil and pulled the trigger but it just went click.

"Guess I forgot to load it," said the Devil. He grinned. "It takes magic bullets. And look what I found."

He held up a magazine. It was Today's Wizard. "Thanks for the tip, Clyde," he said.

Billy was shocked. "You told on him!" he said. He pulled Clyde's string.

"I'm sorry!" said Clyde. "Pull my string again. But only halfway out this time."

"Don't do it!" said the Devil. But Billy did.

"Si vis pacem para bellum," said Clyde. "Bibere venenum in auro."

The Devil stood up, looking scared. And no wonder: three gold bullets had appeared in Billy's gun.

"I was just about to leave," said the Devil. He held the magazine over his face and tried to hide.

But it did him no good. Billy shot him three times: once in the snout and twice in the heart.

The Devil disappeared. So did the magic gun. Only the magazine was left. Billy picked it up.

It had a hole all the way through it. "Oh no," said Billy. He opened it with trembling hands.

The Wizard's pointy hat had a big hole in it but the Wizard was okay.

"Good going, Billy," he said. "You're no sissy. But how did the Devil find me?"

Billy told him and turned the page.

"That Clyde," the Wizard said. "He can't keep his big mouth shut. Pull his string and let's see what he has to say for himself."

Billy pulled Clyde's string.

"I'm sorry," said Clyde. "The Devil said he would make me a Devil too. Anything is better than being a doll. Almost."

"We all make mistakes," said the Wizard. "So I forgive you. Besides, you saved the day."

"It's true," said Billy. "Maybe the Wizard will make you into a little boy, as a reward."

"Thanks anyway," said Clyde. "I'd rather be a doll."

Billy thought about that.

"Suit yourself," said the Wizard. "I'm out of here."

"What about your hat?" Billy asked the Wizard. "It has a hole in it."

"I have an extra," said the Wizard. He was starting to fade away. "And now I don't have to hide anymore."

Billy turned the page. The pointy hat was still there but the Wizard was gone.

"What's that infernal racket?" said Billy's father. He was standing in the door. "Give me that magazine and go back to bed."

"Yes, sir," said Billy. He handed his father the magazine.

"Today's Wizard," said Billy's father. He threw it onto the pile. "Pointy hats and dolls! You are such a sissy. Go back to bed and take your doll with you."

"Yes, sir," said Billy. He pulled Clyde's string as he went into the house.

"You're the big sissy," said Clyde.

"What did you say?" asked Billy's father.

"Nothing," said Billy. "It wasn't me."

Billy and the Pond Vikings

Billy had a grandfather. His grandfather had a pond. It was in his back yard.

One day Billy saw a little boat floating on the pond. It had a square sail and lots of little oars.

It was filled with little men.

"Cool boat," said Billy. It had a dragon head on the front.

"We are the Pond Vikings," said the little men. Billy had to lean way down to hear them. "Come and sail with us. We are going to kill frogs with our axes."

"But frogs are nice," said Billy.

"No, they are not," said the Pond Vikings. "They are green."

Billy thought about that.

"Your boat is too little anyway," Billy said. It was smaller than his shoe.

"It's not a boat, it's a Viking ship," said the Pond Vikings. "It just looks little because you are too big. If you step on board you will see that it is just the right size for killing frogs."

Billy thought about that.

"Unless you are a big sissy," said the Pond Vikings.

Billy stepped on board the Viking ship. As soon as his shoe touched the deck he became very small. The Pond Vikings all wore helmets with horns on them. They wore fur vests. They had yellow beards and axes.

They gave Billy an axe and a long oar. "You have to help us row," they said.

It was a long way across the pond. Billy got tired and his hands hurt. He began to cry.

The Pond Vikings just laughed. "You're a crybaby," they said. They took away his axe but they made him keep his oar.

Billy wished he had never stepped on board.

They made Billy row until they found a frog. It was sitting on a lily pad. It was bigger than the Pond Vikings, but there were more of them. They killed it with their axes. The blood made the water pink.

Billy felt sorry for the frog. "Are you going to eat it?" he asked.

"No," said the Pond Vikings. "We just like to kill things. We don't eat them."

"What do you eat?' Billy asked. He was hungry.

"Viking food," they said. They gave Billy some. It wasn't very good but they made him eat it.

After a while it got dark and Billy started to cry again. The Pond Vikings just laughed.

The next day they rowed across the pond again. They killed another frog with their axes. The blood made the water pink.

Billy felt sorry for the frogs. He hated the Pond Vikings. He didn't like their food, either.

"I don't want to be a Viking," said Billy. "I want to go home."

"You should have thought of that before you stepped on board," they said.

They made Billy row even though his hands were sore.

They saw three frogs sitting on a big lily pad. The Pond Vikings snuck up on them from behind. The Viking ship didn't make any noise.

Just when they were about to attack, Billy shouted, "Look out!"

The frogs turned around. They had big green eyes. They saw the Pond Vikings just in time.

The Vikings jumped out with their axes but the frogs killed them with their teeth. The blood made the water pink.

Then they sank the Viking ship.

They didn't kill Billy, though. "You are our friend," they said. They could talk. "You helped us and now we will help you."

"I'm hungry," said Billy. "I want to go home."

The frogs gave Billy a fly to eat. Billy had never eaten a fly before. It was as big as a chicken.

"I didn't know that frogs had teeth," said Billy.

"We keep them a secret," said the frogs. "They are for getting even."

Billy thought about that.

The frogs were green but Billy liked them. They liked Billy, too. They gave him a ride on their backs to the edge of the pond.

"Just step ashore," said the frogs. "You will be big again."

As soon as he stepped ashore, Billy was as big as a little boy again. It was like magic.

"Thank you," said Billy as the frogs jumped away.

They were small again. They couldn't talk anymore. They just croaked.

"I was worried about you," said Billy's grandfather. "You were gone all night."

"I was sailing with the Pond Vikings," Billy said. "There was no wind and they made me row. My hands are sore."

He showed his grandfather.

Billy's grandfather was a doctor. He fixed Billy's hands. "Make-believe is fun for little boys," he said. "But you must never step on board a Viking ship."

"I've learned my lesson," said Billy.

Billy's grandfather patted him on the head. Billy hated that but he didn't say anything. He was still hungry.

In the house, it was time for supper. Billy's father was sitting at the table waiting to be fed. He was out of jail again. He was reading the paper.

"Get a load of this," he said. "'Frogs Endangered by Vikings'."

"Perhaps that explains why my pond is so pink," said Billy's grandfather.

"Frogs are nice," said Billy.

"No they are not," said Billy's father. "They are green."

"They have teeth," said Billy. "For getting even."

Billy's grandmother was dead so Billy's grandfather cooked supper. "What's this?" asked Billy.

It was frog legs.

Billy didn't want any. Instead, he ate flies. He caught them between his fingers and stuck them to his tongue. There were lots of flies in the kitchen.

"I've never seen a little boy do that before," said Billy's grandfather.

"That Billy's crazy," said Billy's father.

"That's what you think," said Billy.

"That's what you think sir," said Billy's father.

"Sir," said Billy. He ate more flies. He was very very hungry and it took lots of flies to fill him up.
It was good to be home.

Billy and the Time Skateboard

"Go out and play with your friends," said Billy's mother.

"I don't have any friends," said Billy.

"You can make friends," said Billy's mother. "Here's a dollar."

Billy went out to play. He didn't have any friends. He had one enemy, though. His name was Vernon. Vernon lived next door.

Billy looked over the fence. "Want to play with me?" he asked.

Vernon was in a wheelchair. He made a face. "No, because you're stupid," he said. "I'd rather play with a girl."

"I'll give you a dollar," said Billy.

"Let me see it," said Vernon.

Billy showed him the dollar.

"I'd like to have a dollar," said Vernon. "Give it to me and I will let you ride on my skateboard."

"It doesn't have any wheels," said Billy.

"It doesn't need wheels," said Vernon. "It's a Time Skateboard."

"There's no such thing," said Billy.

"There is so," said Vernon. "Try it."

Billy gave Vernon the dollar. Vernon gave Billy the skateboard. He handed it over the fence.
Billy got on it but he couldn't make it go. "It doesn't work," he said. "I want my dollar back."
"Maybe it needs batteries," said Vernon. "It's my dollar now."
He rolled away laughing.

Billy hated Vernon.
He turned the skateboard over. It looked stupid. Instead of wheels it had a place for batteries.
Billy went into the house and stole two batteries out of his mother's purse. It was filled with batteries.
He put two batteries in the skateboard and pointed it toward the past. Then he got on.
It took off real fast. When it stopped, Billy lost his balance. He fell off in the mud. There was a big battle all around.
Bullets were whizzing through the air. Dead bodies were all around.
There was a man in a blue suit with gold buttons. "Who are you?" Billy asked.
"I am Napoleon," said the man. "What is that thing?"
Billy told him: "A Time Skateboard."
"Just what I need," said Napoleon. He grabbed it and Billy started to cry.
"Don't be such a crybaby," said Napoleon. Bullets were whizzing all around.
Billy got mad. "It's mine," he said. "I gave a dollar for it."
He grabbed it back. He pointed it toward the future and got on.
It took off real fast and Napoleon disappeared.

When it stopped, Billy fell off on the concrete. There were rocket ships all around. They were shooting at each other. There were robots, too. They were all fighting.

One of the robots saw Billy and whirred over. It tried to kill Billy with a ray gun, but Billy got away just in time.

He fell off the skateboard into the grass. It was wet and smelled funny.

Now Billy was in the woods. There were cave men all around. They had big spears. They grabbed Billy and tied him up with leather strings.

"I'm just a little boy," said Billy. But it didn't do any good.

The cave men couldn't talk. They were going to eat Billy. His legs were tied together with leather strings and he couldn't run.

The cave men were building a fire. They were using sticks.

Billy hopped over to the skateboard and got on when they weren't looking. It took off real fast.

The cave men disappeared. When the skateboard stopped, Billy fell off again. He was back in his yard.

He untied his legs and threw the leather strings away. The cave men didn't know any good knots.

Vernon was looking through the fence. He couldn't look over it because his wheelchair was too short.

"I want my dollar back," said Billy. "I don't like this Time Skateboard."

"Who cares," said Vernon. "Besides, you have already used it. I don't like used stuff."

He rolled away laughing.

Billy had an idea.

He took out one of the batteries and pointed the skateboard toward the past. He got back on it with one foot and made it go just a little.

He didn't fall off this time. He stepped off and the skateboard disappeared.

He looked over the fence. Now Vernon was holding the skateboard in his lap.

Billy was holding the dollar. He showed it to Vernon.

"I'd like to have a dollar," said Vernon. "Give it to me and I will let you ride on my skateboard."

"It doesn't have any wheels," said Billy.

"It doesn't need wheels," said Vernon.

"Then you don't need a dollar," said Billy, as he walked away laughing.

He had won. He had his dollar back. Now maybe he could find a real friend.

Billy and the Talking Plant

One day Billy got sent to the office. The principal said, "Run home, Billy. Your grandfather has fallen down dead."

Billy ran home. It wasn't very far.

His grandfather was on the floor in the living room, but he wasn't dead yet.

"He wants to watch TV while he passes away," said Billy's mother.

"They should call it the dying room," said Billy's grandfather. He was always making jokes.

He had a big Harley. He wore a black leather jacket that said Bikers for Christ on the back, and he gave Billy a Savings Bond every year for his birthday.

Billy didn't like Savings Bonds but he liked his grandfather. "Don't die yet," he said.

"Not till this show is over," said Billy's grandfather. Jerry Springer was on. It was like school. They wouldn't stay in their seats.

"My time is almost up, Billy," said Billy's grandfather. It was during a commercial. "I am leaving you my colors."

He handed Billy his jacket. "It's too big for me," said Billy.

"You'll get bigger," said his grandfather. "And I have something else for you."

"What?" asked Billy. He hoped it wasn't a Savings Bond. Maybe it would be the big Harley!

"My plant," said Billy's grandfather. Billy was disappointed. The plant was in a little pot on the coffee table.

"I want you to take care of it for me while I am dead," said Billy's grandfather.

That seemed like a long time. "Won't that be forever?" asked Billy.

"Not if Jesus has anything to say about it," said Billy's grandfather. "We will all be raised from the dead very soon, and I will want my plant. You can keep the jacket."

As soon as the show was over, he died.

Billy's mother closed his eyes with the remote because she didn't like to touch dead people. Billy just watched.

She used it like a little stick.

Billy put the plant in his room. It had big green leaves.

After a few days the leaves started to droop. Billy was afraid it would die.

He stole a dollar from his mother's purse and went to the magazine store. Billy liked magazines.

"Do you have any magazines about plants?" he asked the store owner. He showed him the dollar.

"You're in luck,' said the store owner. He took the dollar and gave Billy a copy of Plants Magazine.

Billy took the magazine home. He looked at all the pictures. None of them looked like his grandfather's plant. The leaves were the right color but the wrong shape.

He took the magazine to the store and tried to get his money back.

"All sales final," said the store owner. "Try the little ads in the back. It may be that you might find just what you are looking for there."

When Billy got home, the plant looked even worse. Its leaves were turning yellow.

Billy looked in the back of the magazine. There was a little ad that said Teach your plant to talk. One dollar.

There was a box number.

Billy stole a dollar from his mother's purse and sent it to the box number. He stole a stamp too.

The next day a little stick came in the mail. It looked like a popsicle stick.

The instructions said, Stick in dirt next to plant. Wait one hour.

Billy stuck the stick in the dirt and went out to play.

After an hour he went back inside. He closed the door of his room and the plant said, "Water."

"What?" said Billy.

"Water," said the plant.

Billy gave it some water. He waited for the plant to say something else.

It didn't, so he went back out to play.

The next morning the plant looked better. Its leaves were drooping less but they were still yellow. It said, "Water."

Billy gave it some water and went to school. When he got home, the plant said "Water" again.

"Is that all you can say?" asked Billy.

"I'm a plant," said the plant. "I don't have to say anything at all."

Billy thought about that. He gave it some water and went out to play.

The next morning, the plant was green again. And it didn't droop at all. Billy was glad.

"Take me to school," the plant said.

Billy took the plant to school.

"You can't bring a plant to school," said the teacher.

"It's a talking plant," said Billy.

"Prove it," said the teacher.

"Say water," said Billy. He was talking to the plant. The plant said, "Water."

"That's clever," said the teacher. "You can bring it to the Science Fair tomorrow."

That night at supper, Billy said, "There's a Science Fair at school tomorrow."

"Eat your turkey," said Billy's mother. They had turkey every night.

"I'm going to win the Science Prize," said Billy. "I have a talking plant."

"When your father gets out of jail, he will be proud," said Billy's mother.

That night Billy made a sign for the Science Fair. It said Talking Plant.

He used a Magic Marker from his mother's purse. It was filled with them.

Billy took the plant to the Science Fair at school. He wore his grandfather's jacket.

"You can't wear that at school," said the teacher.

"It was my grandfather's," said Billy. "He had a big Harley."

"You can't wear that at school," said the teacher. "It says Christ on it."

Billy hung it up in the cloak room. It was too big anyway.

The Science Fair was in the gym.

Billy put the plant on the long table. He put the Talking Plant sign in front of it.

The teachers were the judges. They walked by and read the sign. "Let's hear it talk," they said.

"Say water," said Billy.

The plant said, "Water."

The teachers all gathered around. They were all dressed alike. "Make it say water again," they said.

"Water," said the plant. Billy didn't have to ask.

The teachers picked up the pot and looked for a speaker. They couldn't find one.

They frowned and shook their heads. "Ventriloquism is not science," they said.

"What's ventriloquism?" asked Billy.

"It means you are making it talk."

"I am not," said Billy. "It's the stick."

"Prove it," said the teachers.

Billy pulled the stick out. The plant didn't say anything.

"See?" said Billy.

"A plant that doesn't talk doesn't prove anything," said the teachers. "You are disqualified."

"What's disqualified?" asked Billy.

"It means you don't get the Science Prize."

Billy thought about that. It made him mad. He stuck the stick back in the dirt.

"Fuck you," said the plant.

"What?" said the teachers.

"Fuck a bunch of teachers," said the plant.

The teachers sent Billy home. They made him take his plant and his jacket with him.

"What happened?" asked Billy's mother.

"Nothing," said Billy. "We got out early."

He took the plant to his room and put it on his desk.

"You can't say fuck in school," he said. "Even a plant should know that."

"I can say anything I want to," said the plant. "I'm a plant."

Billy thought about that.

"Water," said the plant.

Billy gave it some water and went out to play. He was glad to be home from school.

That night Billy's father was reading the paper. He was home from jail.

"Get a load of this," he said. "'Plant Says Fuck at School'."

"Don't say fuck at the table," said Billy's mother.

"You shut up," said Billy's father.

"That was my plant," said Billy. "I'm taking care of it for grandfather."

"That's my boy," said Billy's father. "I'm taking care of his big Harley. I am proud of you. Be sure and give it plenty of water."

"Did that," said Billy.

Billy and the Magic Midget

One day Billy saw a giant. He was playing in the driveway and it was coming down the street.

Billy ran into the house. He was afraid of giants.

"It's a pretty day," said Billy's mother. "Play outside."

"I am afraid," said Billy. "There is a giant coming down the street. It will get me."

"Giants are make-believe," said Billy's mother.

"This one's not," said Billy. "It's taller than the trees."

"Go play outside," said Billy's mother. "I have to clean the house. Your father is coming home from jail today."

Billy went back outside. The giant was still coming down the street. It wasn't as big as before but it was still bigger than the houses.

Billy ran to the back yard. He tried to hide in the sandbox but the sides were too low.

The giant saw him. It turned in the driveway.

"Go away," said Billy. "This is my yard."

"So what," said the giant. It was wearing yellow pants.

Billy hid behind the garbage can.

"I can see you," said the giant. "Come out."

"Go away," said Billy. He threw a rock at the giant. It just bounced off.

"Stop that," said the giant.

The giant kept coming. It got smaller as it got closer. It wasn't even as tall as the garbage can.

It wasn't a giant at all. It was a midget. "Come out, Billy," it said.

Billy came out from behind the garbage can. He wasn't afraid of midgets.

"I was hiding," said Billy. "I thought you were a giant."

"That's because I was far away," said the midget.

"But things look smaller when they are far away," said Billy. He had noticed this.

"That's most things," said the midget. "Midgets are already small enough, so we stay the same. Everything else looks smaller. It makes us look big."

Billy thought about that. "How come you know my name?" he asked.

"Lots of stupid little boys are named Billy," said the midget.

"How come you are wearing yellow pants?" asked Billy.

"I'm a magic midget," said the midget.

"Prove it," said Billy.

The midget did a magic trick.

"Cool," said Billy.

Billy and the midget played in the sandbox. Billy had never played with a magic midget before. It was fun.

The midget did the magic trick again. "Cool," said Billy.

It started to rain. The sand was getting wet. "Let's go play in your castle," said Billy.

"I don't have a castle," said the midget. "That's giants that have castles. Let's play in the house instead."

Billy went to the back door. "It's raining," he said.

"Then you can play in your room," said Billy's mother. "But the giant has to stay outside."

"It's not a giant," said Billy. "It's a midget. It just looks big because it's far away."

"Most things look smaller when they are far away," said Billy's mother. The midget was standing by the sandbox.

"Midgets don't," said Billy. "They are already small enough. And it's raining."

"I don't care," said Billy's mother. "He can go play in his castle."

"Midgets don't have castles," said Billy. "That's giants that have castles."

"No midgets in the house," said Billy's mother.

Billy went to play in his room. There was nothing to do. He sat on his bed.

"Let me in," said the midget. It was looking in the window. Its face was as big as the window.

"You are too big," said Billy.

"That's because you are all the way across the room," said the midget. "Come over here and you will see."

Billy went to the window and the window got big. The midget was small again. It was standing on the garbage can.

"Open the window," it said.

Billy opened the window and the midget climbed in. Billy had to help. They played for a while but it wasn't as much fun as before.

"Do another magic trick," said Billy.

The midget did. It was the same trick as before.

"Is that the only one you know?"

"That's twice as many as you know," said the magic midget.

Billy's mother knocked on the door. "What's going on in there?" she asked.

"Nothing," said Billy.

"You have to clean your room," she said. "Your father is coming home from jail today."

"I have to clean my room," said Billy.

"That's easy," said the midget. He gave Billy a magic mop. Soon the room was clean, in an instant.

"Cool," said Billy. He liked the midget again. "Now we can play."

"I don't want to play with you anymore," said the midget. "I want to watch TV."

"There's nothing on," said Billy. His feelings were hurt.

"I don't care," said the midget. "I like TV anyway."

The midget went into the living room, where the TV was. When Billy's mother saw it coming, she screamed.

Then it got closer and she saw that it was small.

"Go outside," she said. "I have to clean the house. Billy's father is getting out of jail today."

"I don't care," said the midget. "I want to watch TV." It sat on the couch and picked up the remote.

"Why is he wearing yellow pants?" asked Billy's mother.

"He's a magic midget," said Billy. "Look." He gave his mother the magic mop.

Soon the house was clean. "Now can we watch TV?" asked Billy. He was sitting on the couch beside the magic midget. They were both the same size.

"No," said Billy's mother. "Play outside. It's not raining anymore."

The midget made Billy's mother disappear. "Now we can watch TV," it said.

"I thought you didn't know any more tricks," said Billy.

"That's not a trick," said the midget. "Show me how to work the remote."

They watched TV for a while. There was nothing on but the midget didn't care. "I like TV," it said.

After a while Billy got hungry. "Make my mother appear again," he said.

"Mothers are just make-believe," said the midget.

"No they're not," said Billy. "And there's nothing on anyway."

"Go play in your room," said the midget. It was working the remote. He didn't care if anything was on or not.

Billy played in his room by himself. He didn't like the midget anymore.

Soon Billy's father came home. He was out of jail.

"Where's your mother?" he asked.

"A magic midget has taken over the house," said Billy. "That's him in the yellow pants."

"He's too big for a midget," said Billy's father.

"That's because he's all the way across the room," said Billy. "He looks smaller when you get up close. Try it."

Billy's father tried it. "You're right," he said. "Does your mother know he's here?"

"He made her disappear," said Billy.

"How'd he do that?" asked Billy's father.

"He's a magic midget," said Billy.

"You two shut up," said the midget. "I am trying to watch TV."

"I'm hungry," said Billy's father. "Did your mother leave anything to eat?"

"I don't think so," said Billy. "She was cleaning the house."

"Look in the kitchen," said the midget.

Billy and his father looked in the kitchen. There was a magic pot on the stove. It was filled with beans.

"We had beans in jail," said Billy's father. "I was looking forward to turkey."

"You two shut up," said the midget. "I am trying to watch TV."

"You shut up yourself," said Billy's father. He'd had enough.

He jumped on the midget and tried to get the remote, but the midget was too strong and wouldn't let go.

After a while, Billy's father gave up.

"You never should have let that midget into the house," he said to Billy. They were in the kitchen eating beans.

"He came in the window," said Billy. "It wasn't my fault."

"It was so," said Billy's father. "Now I'm going to have to kill him."

"Good idea," said Billy. He was glad his father was home.

Billy's father sprinkled poison on the beans and gave some to the magic midget. "Here," he said. "Make yourself at home."

He was only pretending to be friendly.

The magic midget ate the beans but didn't die. Instead he smacked his mouth.

"Poison doesn't hurt me," he said. "I'm a magic midget."

"We'll have to think of something else," said Billy's father.

He got his gun out of the closet. It was on a shelf. Billy wanted to help. He got his bow and arrow.

They tried to sneak up on the midget. It was sitting on the couch watching TV. But it saw them just in time.

The magic midget made the bullets miss. Soon the gun was empty. Billy's arrow just bounced off.

"We'll have to think of something else," said Billy's father. "Meanwhile let's watch TV."

They sat and watched TV with the magic midget. Billy hated him but the midget didn't care.

The news was on. "Get a load of this," said Billy's father.

"A midget ran away from the circus today," said the TV. "A reward is offered."

"That's you," said Billy's father. There was a picture of the midget on TV.

"It is not," said the magic midget.

"It is so," said Billy's father. "I can tell by the yellow pants."

"Lots of midgets wear yellow pants," said the midget.

"He's lying," said Billy's father. "I know that's him. I'm calling the circus."

"Good idea," said Billy.

They were whispering so the midget couldn't hear.

Billy's father called the circus. He pretended he was in the kitchen eating beans. "These beans are good," he said, so the midget could hear.

"Shut up," said the midget. "I'm trying to watch TV."

Pretty soon the circus came. They knocked down the door. The midget tried to run but they had a net. They caught him in the back yard. He was trying to hide behind the garbage can.

His magic didn't work in the net. Billy made a face at him.

"He likes to watch TV," said the circus men. They put him in their wagon. It had a circus design on it.

"I helped you capture him," said Billy's father. "What about my reward?"

"What about my mother?" asked Billy.

"First things first," said Billy's father. He held up the reward. It was circus tickets.

Billy had never been to the circus before.

It was neat. There were elephants and clowns and everything.

Then he saw the magic midget, way down in the ring. It looked small in the circus, even far away. It was chained to the monkeys.

"That's him in the yellow pants," said Billy's father.

"He looks stupid," said Billy. He hated the midget.

The clowns made Billy's father laugh. "There are no clowns in the jail," he said. Then the midget did a magic trick. "I almost wish I had gotten to know him better," said Billy's father.

Billy had seen the trick before. The circus made him sad. "I miss my mother," he said.

"Don't be such a crybaby," said Billy's father.

The circus went on and on. The clowns were doing the same stuff over and over. Billy was getting bored.

Then a beautiful woman appeared on the trapeze and did a trick. Then she rode on a horse standing up. The circus was almost over.

"Get a load of her," said Billy's father. "She looks almost sexy in those yellow tights."

"Mother!" shouted Billy. It was his mother.

She heard him. She jumped off the horse and ran up into the stands and gave Billy a big hug. Everybody clapped. They all thought it was part of the show.

"That midget made me appear in the circus," she whispered. "Help me escape."

Billy hid her under the seat so no one noticed. It was made of boards.

"The circus is stupid," she whispered. "I want to go home."

"Me too," said Billy.

"You two shut up," said Billy's father. He was still laughing at the clowns.

Finally the circus was over. Everybody walked out of the tent. Billy made a face at the midget but it was too far away to notice.

Billy didn't care. He went home with his mother and father.

"You should never have let that midget into the house," said Billy's mother when they got home.

"It wasn't my fault," said Billy.

"It was so," said his father. "But you are just a little boy and you didn't know any better."

"I do now," said Billy.

"Billy thought it was a giant," said Billy's mother. "It looked big at a distance."

"That's the problem with midgets," said Billy's father. "What's for supper?"

"Hang on," said Billy's mother and disappeared into the kitchen. She was still wearing her yellow tights. "It's a surprise."

It was cotton candy!

Billy and the Flying Saucer

"Hey, Billy!" said Vernon. "Guess what."

Vernon was the boy next door. Billy looked over the fence.

"What," said Billy. He hated Vernon.

"I have a present for you," said Vernon. He held up a cigarette.

"Cigarettes are bad for you," said Billy.

"No, they are good for you," said Vernon. "You got it backwards. That's because you are stupid."

"No I'm not," said Billy. But he wasn't sure.

"Plus they are cool," said Vernon. He gave the cigarette to Billy. "Smoke it."

Billy smoked it. He knew how from TV. Then he puked on his shoe.

"Here's another cigarette," said Vernon. "You have two shoes."

"Eat your turkey," said Billy's mother. It was supper time.

"I'm not hungry," said Billy. "I smoked two cigarettes today."

"Where did you get them?"

"Vernon gave them to me," said Billy.

"That Vernon," said Billy's mother. "Cigarettes are bad for you."

"I thought so," said Billy. Vernon was a big liar.

"Eat your turkey anyway," said Billy's mother. They had turkey every night.

Billy ate his turkey anyway. Then he watched TV and went to bed.

Soon he had to puke again.

He was afraid to mess up the covers so he puked in the helmet that he kept under his bed. Then he closed his eyes but he couldn't sleep.

He wanted a cigarette.

First thing in the morning, Billy went to the back yard and looked over the fence.

"Looking for something?" Vernon asked. He was smiling.

"A cigarette," said Billy.

"I thought so," said Vernon. "Now you are hooked. Now you have to do anything I say."

"No I don't," said Billy.

"Yes you do," said Vernon. "Say please."

"Please," said Billy.

"See?" said Vernon. He gave Billy a cigarette. This time Billy didn't puke.

That afternoon Billy wanted another cigarette. He looked over the fence and said please.

"Say pretty please," said Vernon.

"Pretty please," said Billy.

"Sorry," said Vernon. He held up a cigarette and broke it in two. He had a whole pack.

Vernon was mean. Billy hated him.

Billy had an idea. "I will trade you my helmet," he said.

"What helmet?"

"It's a Dale Earnhardt helmet," said Billy. "It has a number 3 on it."

"Let's see it," said Vernon.

Billy ran into the house and got the helmet. It still had puke in it. It hadn't dried up yet.

"Here," said Billy. He handed the helmet over the fence. It was black.

"Earnhardt was one of the Greats," said Vernon. "Not stupid like you."

He gave Billy a cigarette and then he put the helmet on his head.

The puke ran down over his face. It was yellow.

Vernon got mad. "Now I'm going to kill you," he said.

"You can't," said Billy. "You can't get over the fence."

It was true. Vernon didn't have any feet. He couldn't get over the fence. Instead he rolled back and forth in his wheelchair.

Billy was glad the fence was there.

That night Billy shook so hard that his bed rattled. He wanted a cigarette.

"What's that noise?" asked Billy's mother.

"Nothing," said Billy. He couldn't let his mother know that he was hooked.

The next morning Billy wanted a cigarette worse than ever. He looked over the fence and there was Vernon. He was rolling up and down in his stupid wheelchair.

"No more cigarettes for Billy," he said. "No more cigarettes for Billy." He was singing it.

Billy pretended to be sorry. "I'm sorry, Vernon," he said. "Please."

Vernon just smiled and shook his head. He was wearing the helmet. He had wiped the puke off his face.

"Pretty please," said Billy. He hated Vernon but he was hooked.

"I feel like reading a magazine," said Vernon.

Billy ran into the house and got a magazine. It was his mother's. He handed it over the fence to Vernon.

Vernon made a face. "This one is all about crime," he said. He threw it down and rolled back and forth over it. "I want one with girls in it."

Billy stole a dollar out of his mother's purse and ran to the magazine store. He needed a cigarette bad.

"The ones with girls are two dollars," said the store owner.

"I only have a dollar," said Billy.

"Then you're out of luck," said the store owner.

Billy waited until the store owner wasn't looking and stole a magazine with girls in it. He ran back home and handed it over the fence to Vernon.

"Now give me my cigarette," Billy said. He held out two fingers. He had seen that on TV.

Vernon shook his head. He was wearing the helmet. "These girls are all standing around," he said. "I want one with girls in wheelchairs."

He threw the magazine down and rolled back and forth over it. Then he threw it back over the fence.

Billy picked up the magazine and ran back to the store.

He had to have a cigarette bad.

He tried to act cool. "I bought the wrong magazine," he said. "I want to swap it for one with girls in wheelchairs."

"This magazine is no good anymore," said the store owner. "Somebody has rolled over it. Besides, you didn't buy it anyway. You stole it."

Billy was shaking all over. He tried to lie. "I paid for it," he said. "You just forgot."

"Store owners don't forget things," said the store owner. "I'm calling the police."

"I'm just a little boy," said Billy. "My father's a policeman."

"No, he's not," said the store owner. "He's in jail."

"He's undercover," said Billy.

"You are a big liar," said the store owner. He took out a cell phone. "Now I'm calling the FBI."

The store owner made Billy wait while he called the FBI. Billy was shaking all over.

"Can I have a cigarette?" he asked.

"You must be hooked," said the store owner. "No smoking in the store."

The store owner was smoking, though. He blew smoke in Billy's face and smiled.

He was as mean as Vernon.

Pretty soon the FBI arrived. They arrived in a helicopter. They were about to handcuff Billy when a flying saucer flew over the town.

It was flying low. Everybody looked up. The FBI and the store owner too. That was their mistake.

The saucer had a Forgetting Ray. It made the FBI forget about taking Billy to jail.

Billy ran home. He was breathing a sigh of relief all the way.

"Where's my magazine?" asked Vernon.

"I forgot it," said Billy.

"Then no cigarette for you."

"I don't care," said Billy. "I don't want one anymore. That flying saucer made me forget I was hooked. It had a Forgetting Ray."

"I saw the flying saucer too," said Vernon. "How come I didn't forget I'm in a wheelchair?"

"That's because you don't have any feet," said Billy. "I want my Dale Earnhardt helmet back."

Vernon gave Billy his helmet back. Vernon had forgotten it was his. He had even forgotten he was mean.

Billy looked inside the helmet before he put it on. Vernon's mother had cleaned out all the puke. Billy had come out ahead.

"Pass the turkey," said Billy. It was supper time.

"Feeling better?" asked his mother.

"Yes ma'am," said Billy. No more cigarettes for him!

Billy and the Withc

One day Billy's teacher fell over dead. The next day they had a substitute. She had a long pointy chin.

"You have to do what I say," she said.

"No we don't," said Billy. "You are just a substitute."

"Yes you do," the substitute said. "Your old teacher is dead. I am your new teacher."

Billy didn't like her. She was mean.

She made him stay after school.

The next day, there she was again.

"I think she's a witch," Billy said during recess. "Look at her chin."

"Pointy chins don't prove anything," the other kids said. "She's not wearing a witch hat."

"Of course not," said Billy.

The next day, there she was again. Her chin was still pointy. She even had a broom. It was parked in the corner.

"You are a witch," said Billy.

"It's withc," said the substitute. She wrote it on the blackboard: WITHC.

"It is not," said Billy.

"It is so," said the substitute. "Now you have to stay after school for being wrong."

She wrote his name on the blackboard: BILYL.

"That's not even my name," said Billy. "So I don't have to stay after school."

"Yes you do," she said.

"My new teacher is a witch," said Billy. It was supper time. "She even has a broom."

"What about a witch hat?" said Billy's father. "Brooms don't prove anything."

"They do so," said Billy. "It is parked in the corner."

"They do not," said Billy's father.

"Do so," said Billy.

"Go to your room," said Billy's father.

Billy missed his old teacher. She had given him an A in spelling. It was the only A he had ever gotten.

"You can't even spell," Billy said the next day at school. "You're just a substitute."

"It's susbitute," the witch said. She shook her broom at Billy. "Now you have to stay after school."

"The broom proves it," Billy said to the other kids during recess. "She's a witch."

"It's withc," said the other kids. "And brooms don't prove anything. They are for sweeping up."

They would believe anything.

"Late again!" said Billy's mother. "Why did you have to stay after school?"

"Extra credit,'" said Billy. He knew better than to tell the truth.

"Get a load of this," said Billy's father. He was reading the paper. "'Withc Teaches School'."

"It's witch," said Billy.

"It says withc here," said Billy's father. He showed Billy the paper.

"That's spelled wrong," said Billy.

"It is not," said Billy's father.

"Is so," said Billy.

"Go to your room," said Billy's father.

"We want our old teacher back," said Billy, the next day. "She was nicer than you."

"Too bad," said the substitute. "She is dead. Now line up for a Spelling Be."

"It's bee," said Billy.

"Incorrect!" said the witch. "You are the first one out. Sit down."

Billy sat down. The next kid's word was witch. She spelled it withc.

"Correct," said the substitute.

The next kid's word was substitute. He spelled it susbitute.

"Correct," said the witch.

Billy started to cry.

During recess the other kids all laughed at Billy. "Billy is a cry-baybie!" they said.

"It's baby," said Billy. "And she is so a witch."

"It's withc," said the other kids.

Billy had never felt so all alone. "I wish we had our old teacher back."

"So do we all," said the other kids. "But we have to take things as they come. We are just kids."

"Besides," they said. "Our old teacher is dead."

That gave Billy an idea.

"I am going to kill the new teacher," Billy said at supper time. "She's a witch."

"It's withc," said Billy's mother. "You used to be such a good speller."

"You are just a little boy," said Billy's father. "You'll get in trouble if you kill her."

"She's just a substitute," said Billy.

"It's susbitute," said Billy's father.

"Eat your tukrey," said Billy's mother.

"There's no such thing as tukrey," said Billy.

"There is so," said Billy's mother. "We have it every night."

"Is not."

"Go to your room," said Billy's father. "Don't be such a cry-baybie."

The next day Billy brought his bow and arrow to school.

It was against the rules but the substitute didn't know the difference.

He shot her through the head. He waited till no one was looking. She fell over and died immediately.

The arrow was sticking in one ear and out the other. Billy had sharpened it in his pencil sharpener. It was electric.

All the other kids cried. Not Billy, though.

"Who killed the substitute?" asked the Principal. She had come running. "If you don't tell, you will all have to stay after school."

She was mad.

"It was Billy," said the other kids. "He is the only one that didn't cry."

"It wasn't me," said Billy. He was good at lying but the bow and arrow gave him away.

He had to stay after school again.

The next day the old teacher was back. "I was only pretending to be dead," she said. "I needed some time off."

"We had a substitute," said Billy. "Now she is dead."

"She was a withc," said the other kids.

"It's witch," said the old teacher. She wrote it on the blackboard: WITCH.

"Told you," said Billy. All the other kids looked up to him now.

"My old teacher's back," said Billy. "What's for supper?"

"Tukrey," said his mother.

"It's turkey, you ignoramus," said Billy's father.

"I meant turkey," said Billy's mother. "You know we have turkey every night."

"Pass the turkey, please," said Billy, relieved. Things were back to normal!

Billy in Dinosaur City

"Pack up your toys," said Billy's father. "We are moving to Dinosaur City."

"Oh boy," said Billy.

"Oh no," said Billy's mother. She didn't like dinosaurs.

It was a long way to Dinosaur City. As soon as they got there, a dinosaur stepped on the car.

"Oh no," said Billy's mother.

It was all squashed.

"We don't need a car anymore," said Billy's father. "We can ride on a dinosaur."

"Oh boy," said Billy.

They all got on.

"I like this new house," said Billy.

It was bigger than the old one. It was newer than the old one and it was all green.

"It is too green," said Billy's mother.

"You shut up," said Billy's father. "Everything is green here."

Billy's room was green. Billy put his toys away and sat on the bed. There was nothing to do.

"Go out and play," said Billy's mother.

"I don't have any friends," said Billy.

"You never did have any friends," said Billy's father. "What else is new?"

"You can make friends with the dinosaurs," said Billy's mother. She was trying to make the best of things.

"What if they don't like me?" asked Billy.

"You sound like your mother," said Billy's father.

"It's too pretty to play inside," said Billy's mother. She was always saying that.

Billy went out to play with the dinosaurs.

But they didn't know how to play. They were way too big.

All they did was stomp on things. They tried to stomp on Billy but he stepped aside just in time. Finally it was supper time.

"Make any friends?" asked Billy's father.

"No," said Billy.

"I thought not," said Billy's father.

"Eat your turkey," said Billy's mother.

"This doesn't taste like turkey," said Billy. "It's too green."

"That does it," said Billy's mother. "I want to go home."

"Shut up, both of you," said Billy's father. He was trying to read his paper.

The next day Billy went to dinosaur school. It was horrible. Even the teacher was a dinosaur.

There weren't any chairs. The dinosaurs never sat down. They just stomped around.

At recess, Billy tried to make friends. "My name is Billy," he said.

"So what," said the dinosaurs. They didn't have names. They tried to stomp on him and he stepped aside, just in time.

Billy was glad when school was out. He walked home alone. He had to be careful because of the dinosaurs.

"I hate school," said Billy when he got home.

"You always hated school," said Billy's father. "What else is new?"

"Try and learn some dinosaur games," said Billy's mother. She was trying to make the best of things.

"They don't play games," said Billy. "They just stomp on things."

"Let's go for a ride," said Billy's father. He folded up his newspaper.

They went for a ride around Dinosaur City. They rode in a little green wagon. There was nothing much to see. All the houses were just alike. There was a dinosaur in each one.

They were all sleeping. Dinosaurs sleep a lot.

"Careful not to wake them up," said Billy's father. "They can be mean when they just wake up."

"They are always mean," said Billy.

"I want to go home," said Billy's mother.

"Shut up, both of you," said Billy's father.

Billy hated Dinosaur City. He played like he was sick so he wouldn't have to go to school.

He waited till his mother wasn't looking and stole a dollar from her purse.

He went to the store to buy a magazine. Billy liked magazines.

"Is this all the magazines you have?" Billy asked the store owner. They were all about dinosaurs.

"What's wrong with dinosaurs?" asked the store owner. He was a dinosaur too.

"Nothing," said Billy. "It's just that I'm interested in other things."

"Try this one," said the store owner. It was called METEOR MAGAZINE.

"Where did you get that magazine?" asked Billy's father. They were having supper.

"It fell from the sky," said Billy.

Billy's father looked at the cover. "That makes sense," he said.

"Eat your brussels sprouts," said Billy's mother.

That night Billy read his magazine. It was pretty stupid. "I'll bet the dinosaurs will like it," he thought.

The next day, Billy took his magazine to school. At recess he showed it to the dinosaurs. He was trying to make friends. This was to be his last attempt.

"Meteors are just big rocks," said the dinosaurs.

"Big rocks in outer space," Billy pointed out.

"Outer space is stupid," said the dinosaurs. They stomped on his magazine and tore it up.

Billy started to cry.

"Now you have to stay after school," said the teacher.

"For what?" Billy asked.

"For being a cry-baby," she said. "Dinosaurs don't cry at recess."

"I'm not a dinosaur," Billy said. "I'm just a little boy."

"That does it," she said. "Now you are expelled."

"For what?" Billy asked.

"For talking back," she said.

"What is expelled?" Billy asked.

"It means you have to go home."

"Oh boy," said Billy.

Billy walked home alone. He hated Dinosaur School. He hated Dinosaur City.

He heard stomping and looked around.

A dinosaur was chasing him! "Wait!" it said. It was waving a piece of paper.

Billy waited. It was too late to run anyway.

"Here's what's left of your magazine," said the dinosaur. It was only one page. "I feel sorry for you."

"Really?" said Billy. No one had ever felt sorry for him before.

"Really," said the dinosaur.

"I guess all dinosaurs aren't bad," said Billy. "Would you like to be my friend?"

"No," said the dinosaur. "I just want to feel sorry for you."

Then it went away.

Billy took what was left of his magazine home. It was only one page. It was filled with little ads.

One ad was for a meteor call. It cost one dollar.

Billy stole a dollar from his mother's purse and sent for it. He stole a stamp too. He waited till she wasn't looking.

"How was school?" asked Billy's mother. They were having supper.

"Okay," said Billy.

"Get a load of this," said Billy's father. He was reading the newspaper. "'Boy Expelled from Dinosaur School.'"

"It wasn't me," said Billy.

"Nobody said it was," said Billy's father. "Pass the brussels sprouts."

"Aren't you going to school?" asked Billy's mother. It was the next morning.

"Of course," said Billy. But he was just pretending. Instead, he hid under the house. There was nothing to do.

Then the mail came. It was his meteor call. Billy had forgotten all about it.

It looked like a whistle except it was big. It came with instructions:

WAIT TILL PARENTS ARE ASLEEP
TAKE TO TOP OF ROOF OR HILL
POINT UP AT SKY AND BLOW

Billy waited until his parents were asleep. Then he took the meteor call to the top of Dinosaur Hill. It was the highest one around.

He pointed the meteor call up at the sky and blew. It made a big loud hooting noise. All the lights in Dinosaur City came on.

"Uh oh," said Billy. Now he was in trouble.

Just then a huge meteor came shooting down from outer space. It almost hit Billy but he stepped aside just in time.

Instead it hit Dinosaur City and squashed all the houses, almost. "Cool," said Billy.

He ran down the hill and looked around. There was a dead dinosaur in each house.

But wait! One dinosaur was still alive, just barely. It was the one that had felt sorry for Billy.

It was bleeding all over. Dinosaur blood is green. It was writhing in agony.

"I feel sorry for you," said Billy.

Then he ran home and went to bed. Luckily, his house was the only one that was not squashed. His parents were still asleep.

"Get a load of this," said Billy's father. It was the next day. He was reading the newspaper. "'Dinosaurs Extinct. Meteor Tragedy Squashes All'."

"What's extinct?" asked Billy.

"It's like expelled," said Billy's father. "They won't be around anymore."

"I am so glad," said Billy's mother. "Now we can move back home again."

"Pack up your toys," said Billy's father.

"Oh boy," said Billy. He packed up his toys. "But I feel sorry for the dinosaurs."

And he did. But only a little.

Info

Terry Bisson is a Science Fiction writer who also writes stories for thoughtful young readers. A native of Kentucky and New York City, he now lives in Oakland, California.

The original appearances of these stories were as follows:

"Billy and the Ants", *Fantasy & Science Fiction*, October 2005

"Billy and the Fairy", *Fantasy & Science Fiction*, May 2006

"Billy and the Bulldozer", *Amazon Short*, December 2005

"Billy and the Unicorn", *Fantasy & Science Fiction*, July 2006

"Billy and the Spacemen", *Fantasy & Science Fiction*, August 2008

"Billy and the Wizard", *Wizards*, edited by Jack Dann & Gardner Dozois (Berkley, 2007)

"Billy and the Talking Plant", *Postscripts*, Autumn 2006

"Billy and the Magic Midget", *Other*, December 2006

"Billy and the Flying Saucer", *ElevenEleven*, 2008, and *Flurb*, Spring, 2009

"Billy and the Pond Vikings", "Billy and the Time Skateboard", "Billy and the Withc" and "Billy in Dinosaur City" are original to *Billy's Book*, (PS, 2009) published in England.

An additional story "Billy and the Circus Girl" appeared in *Flurb*, Fall, 2006, but it was deemed unsuitable to appear anywhere else.

A fugitive Lulu books edition of *Billy's Book* appeared in the U.S. as *Billy's Picture Book* with illustrations by Rudy Rucker in 2011. And in 2020, Rudy republished *Billy's Picture Book* via his Transreal Books, plus an illustrated ebook edition, plus this all-text *Billy's Book* that you hold in your hands.

Finis Coronat Opus.

www.ingramcontent.com/pod-product-compliance
Lightning Source LLC
Chambersburg PA
CBHW060954120626
46557CB00003B/1153